THE WEAVER'S GIFT

THE WEAVER'S GIFT

By KATHRYN LASKY

Photographs by

CHRISTOPHER G. KNIGHT

FREDERICK WARNE

New York   London

Frederick Warne & Co., Inc.
New York, New York
Library of Congress Cataloging in Publication Data
Lasky, Kathryn.
The weaver's gift.
Summary: Describes the many activities that
take place from the time a sheep is sheared until
the fleece is woven into a soft blanket.
1. Textile crafts—Juvenile literature. 2. Wool—
Juvenile literature. [1. Textile crafts. 2. Wool.
3. Handicraft] I. Knight, Christopher G. II. Title.
TT699.L36   746.1   80-12042
ISBN 0-7232-6191-1
Book Design by Kathleen Westray
Printed in the U.S.A. by Maple Press
Binding by A. Horowitz & Son
1 2 3 4 5 84 83 82 81 80

For CAROLYN and MILTON FRYE,
who know the beauty from start to finish

ONE MARCH MORNING

It is the worst sort of a day late in winter. All week long there had been promises of spring and the thaw had turned the barnyard squishy with mud. But last night a freezing cold rain had come — snarling and full of ice.

Winter has to have the last word, and Carolyn Frye feels it as soon as she gets up. She just knows that a lamb has been born on this wet icy cold morning of early March.

Carolyn and her husband, Milton, jump into their "lambing clothes," grab towels, and rush out to the barnyard. There by a fence post, spotted with mud and blood, is a baby lamb, its face wet and blue. There are slivers of ice on its nose and in the corner of its eye is a tiny frozen teardrop. Lambs usually stand immediately after birth, but this one lies in a heap as lifeless as an old sweater tossed in a corner. The mother ewe stands over the lamb trying to lick off the slime of birth, but she cannot lick it fast enough to stop little scales of ice from forming over the small body.

Carolyn knows she must work quickly to save the lamb. Wrapping the newborn in a towel, she scoops it up in her arms. She holds the baby close to her chest and coaxes the ewe toward the barn, speaking softly to her about her baby girl (for the lamb is female) and about warm barns and grain. Leaning into the wind, slowly the three of them make their way across the barnyard. All Carolyn can hear is the sucking noise of the icy mud underneath feet and hooves. All she can feel is the tiny heartbeat against her one hand that she keeps under the towel. All she can think is—*Live!*

Inside the barn it is dark and smells of clean hay and warm animals. Carolyn leads the ewe toward the glow of a corner pen that melts out of the barn's shadows. This is the lambing pen Carolyn had prepared three weeks before, and Milton had turned on the pen's heatlamp first thing this morning.

A lambing pen is a nice place—not too big, not too small, but just right for a ewe and her baby. With lots of clean fresh hay and the heatlamp going, it's a perfect nursery for a newborn lamb.

Now Carolyn begins to rub the lamb quite hard. The ewe helps too, by licking off the slime that is melting under the heatlamp. The slime is not all that is melting. Thin vapors of steam rise from the mother's back, and the faint odor of lanolin oil fills the pen. This ewe is a Merino sheep. Among Merinos the lanolin tends to travel, from pockets under their skin, along the fine fibers or threads of wool and collect on the outer ends, making their fleece dark with oil. As Carolyn continues to rub, the ewe tussles roughly with her newborn — butting and pushing it into breathing. In fifteen minutes the lamb is standing, and a pale pink tinges its nostrils. No more frozen tears.

"Here here here," whispers Carolyn.

"Hey hey hey." That is the ewe making her special sound, a sound ewes make only when their newborns first arrive and never again. Carolyn squeezes some milk from the mother's teat onto her finger and then puts her finger into the lamb's mouth.

"Here here here. Try some, try some. Good milk! Good milk!" In a minute or two Carolyn feels the sure tug of the lamb sucking on her finger and guides its mouth to the mother's teat. The pen swirls with "here here's" and "hey hey's." The newborn lamb is standing and nursing — all by itself.

Lambing is over by early April, but the work of raising sheep and caring for them continues all year long. For instance, during the spring and summer, acres of hay must be grown and cut and baled for the cold months when there is no more pasture for grazing. In early winter, when the snow comes, the sheep are brought in to the enclosed barnyard where Milton and Carolyn can feed them.

And in both the barnyard and the pastures there are always fences to mend to keep predators out and sheep in. A hole in the fence gave one of the sheep, Strawberry, his name. One July he found that hole, wriggled out, went directly to the strawberry patches, and ate them down to the ground.

Sometimes the sheep need special attention. When one ewe's lamb died, Carolyn had to spend hours applying compresses to the ewe's milk bag to stop the milk from coming, for without a nursing lamb her bag had become painfully swollen. And every now and then Milton must clip the sheeps' hooves to prevent splitting. The sheep are not wild. They are domesticated animals and could not survive without Milton and Carolyn's care.

A SHEARING KIND OF DAY

The sun is just reaching over the hills, and in that earliest of morning light the meadows turn almost white, almost incandescent. If you squint your eyes just so, dewdrops and grass blades swirl in a wild silvery dance full of flashes, glints, and slivers of glancing light. But only for a moment, because the sun rises, the dew evaporates, a light wind blows, and it's a shearing kind of day!

Carolyn and Milton have everything ready for the sheep shearer's arrival: the tarp, the buckets of water, the tuna fish sandwiches, the cold beer. Rob Burroughs has been shearing sheep for over fifty years. He is a curiously shaped man. Rugged and built low to the ground, it seems as if his body is forever curved around a sheep for shearing, even when he has just stepped out of his car.

The talk is all sheep talk—there is a double charge for shearing Merinos because of their deep folds of skin, which grow the finest fleece in the world but the hardest fleece to shear.

"Takes a younger feller than me to shear that breed!" Bob says. "Feller down in the next town got a beautiful fleece off a Merino. I say to him, 'If you can get Carolyn Frye to spin this for you, your wife will be some pleased.' . . . Let's get started. Who's our first customer? Not the Merino I hope."

Milton half-carries, half-rides a Romney ewe to the tarp.

"Hello there." Rob greets the ewe and quickly flips her onto her tailbone so that she appears to be sitting down. Turning on the electric shears, Rob bends over her and begins to work. First he runs down the ewe's chest on a diagonal toward the belly. The shears plow gently through the wool as Rob pushes the belly fleece onto the tarp.

"Rob, what's the best breed to shear?" someone asks.

"The quiet breed—ones that lay peaceable."

In seconds the entire belly is cleared of its fleece and the small pockets of lanolin, yellow and pouched, are visible in the crease where the sheep's hind legs join her body. Rob keeps the shears traveling out from the belly, up the right flank. Then he shifts his position and cocks the sheep's head to the left a bit. The day is cool and dry, but Rob is already sweating. It is hard work. It is important that the two-hundred-pound ewe not panic, for otherwise she could be cut by the shears. But Rob is a professional. He knows how to handle sheep, and the ewe will not be hurt at all during the shearing.

"Rob, what does it take to be an expert shearer?"

"Strong back and a weak mind."

His shears begin to move gently across the sheep's cheek. He holds the animal's jaw firmly in one hand. The shears move delicately down the other side of the neck and then up the other cheek. He carefully guides the shears in and around the features of the sheep's face. The shears move smoothly and with all the graceful precision of a figure skater's blades. The woolly overhang of the brow is cut free.

"Hello, Missy!" Rob gently reassures her. The head is shorn. The heavy wise old head has been transformed, and now there is a naked pointy little face with huge bewildered eyes.

The shears travel on: down the other side of the neck, then a straight plunge down the flawless wool of the shoulder and on to the leg. The last bit of wool is separated from the body. The sheep is free, and the fleece lies like a drift of snow around her feet.

"I brought you a sheep and got back a goat, sir!" Milton exclaims as he looks at the scrawny animal before him. The ewe has been left naked. Her skin, showing through pink and rippled with a hint of fuzz, looks exactly like corduroy.

All morning Rob continues shearing without a break. Sheep after sheep. A ram, a male sheep, is shorn and returns to the barnyard. Another newly shorn ram turns to look at him. His gaze is low and deadly.

"Uh oh!" says Milton as the angry ram paws the ground with its hoof. But before Milton can move, the ram is running full speed across the barnyard. There is a sound like distant thunder as the two heads collide. And then Milton, yelling, whooping, hollering, and calling names, roars into the thick of the fight. *Stop it! Stop it!* He whacks the aggressor ram across the face and then grabs the other one and wrestles it toward the gate. The two rams must be separated or else they could kill each other. The aggressor ram does not recognize his old barnyard neighbor who now, pink and naked, seems like a threatening stranger.

Rob keeps working. When the lanolin builds up on his shears, he dips them in the bucket of water to cut the grease.

Most of the sheep are white, but no two fleeces are alike. One fleece is peeled off, leaving what appears to be a huge drift of snow; another lies like a mountain of whipped butter. A charcoal-colored ewe is shorn. The fleece rolls off in great silver waves that shimmer with the vibrations of the electric shears. And a light gray ram is left standing in a tide of Atlantic foam.

Finally, Rob shears the Merino with its deep wrinkles and folds of skin. He shears her without one nick, and when he finishes, the exquisite fleece sets on the tarp looking like great mounds of beaten egg whites. Merino wool is so soft and fine it is often used for baby blankets and baby caps and all kinds of things that touch the skin.

By the end of the morning the sheep are shorn. Their fleeces are piled separately on the lawn, each with a name tag — Amy, Abby, Sontag, Henry, Strawberry, and Daisy. Maverick bits of wool swirl up from the ground, and tufts of poplar seed drift through the air over the piles of wool that float like islands on the grass below. Rob packs his shears, eats his sandwich, and then is on his way to the farm down the road apiece. It's a shearing kind of day.

A LAWNFUL OF WOOL

Under the dappled light of the poplar trees, where the grass is thick and there is no mud, Carolyn spreads the fleece of Henry the Romney ram who was shorn the day before.

It is time to sort the wool and grade it. The poor wool from each fleece must be separated from the good; and the best must be separated from the better. For the job Carolyn has three paper bags, each marked with a letter —A, B, and C.

She begins by *skirting* the fleece, which is done by tearing off the edges that are sticky with dirt and manure. These pieces are sometimes called *tags,* and Carolyn tosses them into the C bag. Some of the poorest wool comes from the legs, hind quarters, belly, and neck of the sheep. Some wool is *weathered,* which means it has been bleached and dried by the sun to an uneven color and texture. It can be a weaver's nightmare to come upon a skein,or coiled length,of weathered wool. Some very particular sheep raisers strap coats onto their herd to avoid weathering the fleece. As Carolyn continues to skirt, the fleece grows smaller and smaller. The C bag, or "tag bag," is almost filled. This poor wool can be washed and used for stuffing.

Carolyn then begins to pull apart the remaining fleece. The wool with the most even color and the tightest curl (or *crimp*), which is the best wool, goes into the *A* bag; what is left over goes into the *B* bag. In twenty minutes Henry's fleece has been sorted and put into three separate bags. Carolyn will wash it a pound at a time in water that is warm but not so hot that the lanolin will be drawn from the wool. It is the lanolin that makes the wool soft.

A PUFF OF SMOKE
YOU CAN HOLD

At Carolyn's feet are two huge wicker baskets. One is empty and the other is filled with clean fleece, great heavy tangled heaps of it. Now that Carolyn has sorted and washed the wool, it is ready to be *carded*.

"You find a pace you'd feel comfortable with for twenty years. Then you can keep it for five hours," she says.

Carolyn presses hanks of wool onto one carding comb, and with that comb held steady against her leg she brushes the wool with the other comb until it begins to straighten out. Then she transfers the wool to the other comb and brushes some more. The rhythm spreads through Carolyn's body, and she hardly needs the song.

In carding, wool is drawn across the teeth of metal carding combs to straighten out the fibers and fluff them up for *spinning*. It takes a long time to card a pound of wool—at least an entire afternoon or evening of steady work. Carding can be boring and even tiring for the muscles in the backs of Carolyn's arms. But if she does not card there is no wool to spin, and if she does not spin there is no yarn to weave or knit. So Carolyn searches for a song — a song in her head that will give an easy rhythm to her hands as she brushes endlessly.

Soon the fibers of wool are straightened and the hank of fleece lies evenly spread like a mist over the surface of the carding comb. By backcombing it Carolyn lifts the mist up from one comb and rolls it on to the other. It rests there a moment—a roll of air and wool.

"A puff of smoke you can hold, that is what a good *rolag* should look like," says Carolyn as she picks it up to show a young neighbor named Max and then puts it into the empty basket by her feet.

By the end of the afternoon the basket is filled with puffs of smoke.

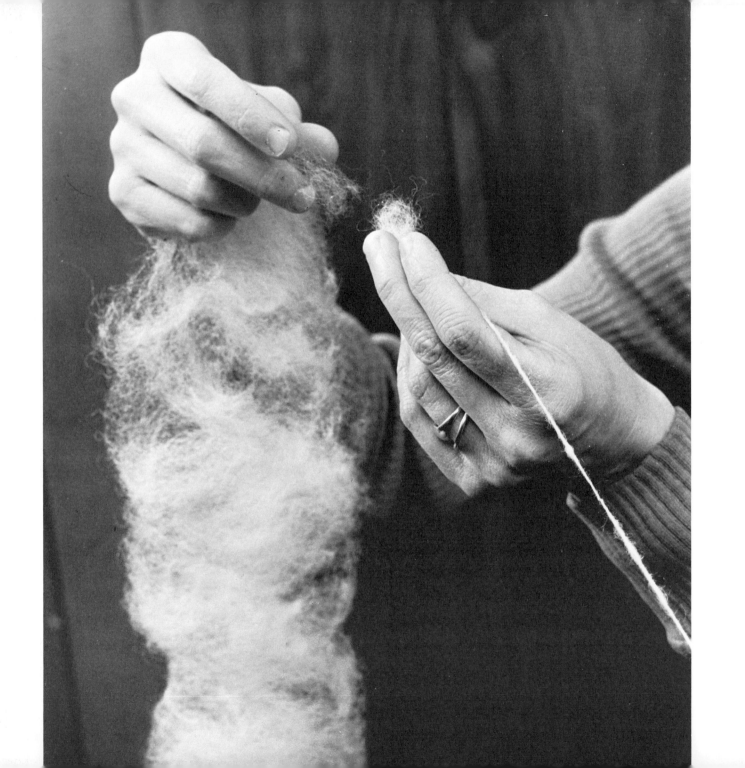

ALMOST MAGIC

The wool is ready for Carolyn to spin into yarn.

A single fiber of wool has countless tiny hooks. In spinning, the individual fibers are twisted so that the hooks interlock into a single strand of yarn. It is the locking hooks that give wool its strength. A good spinner's yarn is light, warm, and strong.

It took Carolyn a long time and much practice to become a good spinner. She bought a book and learned how to thread the rolag through the *bobbin* and how to hold the rolag while spinning and how to work the *treadle* —all at once. She learned about positions for her hands, her feet, her head, and almost every part of her body. And after all this learning, she was still a rotten spinner. Her yarn was weak. It broke. It was always too tight or not tight enough.

Carolyn had read the book, but the book could not tell her about the *rhythms* of spinning. The book could not make her feel the spirit of the wheel or where her body's rhythms and the wheel's might meet to make strong yarn. Every time Carolyn sat down at the wheel she almost cried. She could feel her muscles tense and her stomach twist inside. She even imagined herself just vanishing down the little bobbin hole. She began to hate the wheel.

Then, one day Carolyn went to a county fair. At the fair an older woman was giving a spinning demonstration. Carolyn watched and watched her as she spun. She watched the fluid movement of the woman's back and shoulders as she played the rolag back and forth. The book had taught Carolyn the mechanical steps, but seeing the woman at the fair had given Carolyn a glimpse beyond the steps and the rules into the magical rhythms of spinning. Carolyn went home that day and began spinning. She never had any more problems.

BOBBIN

BOBBIN HOLE

TREADLE

Now she picks up a rolag of her newly carded wool. She draws out some of the fibers from it and presses them onto the yarn already spun that is coming through the bobbin hole on her side — the spinner's side — of the wheel. She holds the rolag firmly in her right hand and begins pumping the treadle. As they are pulled out, the fibers from her right hand form a tiny triangle between Carolyn's hand and the already twisted or spun fibers just inches from her right hand. With her left hand she stops the already spun yarn from twirling up into the triangle of unspun fibers. With her right hand she controls the amount of fiber she lets into the triangle from the rolag. If she wants thick yarn, she lets more fibers from the rolag be drawn into the triangle. If she wants thinner yarn, she lets fewer fibers into the triangle. All of the rolag is pulled toward the bobbin hole and would disappear right down it if Carolyn did not hold the rolag firmly, playing it just so.

Rolag after rolag Carolyn spins into yarn. When a bobbin is full, she winds the yarn onto her *kniddy knoddy* into a skein. There is a special sound to this as the bobbin turns and the wool yarn whispers while passing on to the kniddy knoddy. But the best sound of all is the flutter of the wheel when Carolyn spins. If butterflies had wings of wood as thin as paper and flew in perfect circles, this would be the sound of a spinning wheel.

"Spinning!" says Carolyn. "It's almost magic!"

A BAGFUL OF YELLOW, A BAGFUL OF GREEN

On a forgotten country road, in a damp ditch missed by the sun, grows a plant as old as time—*horsetail.* Once, millions of years ago when the dinosaurs lived, horsetail plants were gigantic and grew everywhere. Now they grow like miniature fir trees, six or eight inches tall and with green needles radiating in circles from their stems. Every June, Carolyn goes to find the plants to make dye for her wool. A paper bag full of horsetail can yield a soft yellow dye with a hint of green.

The other plant that Carolyn looks for early in the season is a fern called *bracken.* If she finds it when it is still summer—young with its fronds or leaves curled tight as baby fists, she will be able to make the prettiest green dye from it.

Near the edge of the woods, amid flashes of Indian paintbrush and bloodroot, Carolyn finds the bracken. But she is too late. The fronds have uncurled and spread, and the fern stands nearly three feet high with a span of two feet. Still, a bagful of bracken handled carefully in the dye pot can give up a warm lime green color.

Carolyn does not dig up the bloodroot, although she could get a bright red-orange from it. "I don't like to use the roots of things. I just don't," she says.

August is the month for dyers. When Carolyn walks through the countryside in August and the world seems to be that inky green of high summer, she knows there is another secret world of color stuff where even the plainest plant can yield the most startling color. A *milkweed,* still podless, holds the promise of green. There are whole fields floating with *Queen Anne's lace* for yellow, *coreopsis* for burnt orange, *marigold* for gold, and *tansy* for another yellow. There are *blueberries* for the softest purple, but Carolyn would rather eat the berries than use them for color. Come fall there will be *butternut* for brown, *sumac* for tan, *onion skins* for rust, and old *tomato vines* for still another shade of green. But in August it is as if fall has already arrived in the eye of Carolyn's mind, for she has a dyer's imagination and can see the hidden colors of deep summer. The only color that Carolyn will not be able to make is red. The only true red to be had comes from a tiny bug, the *cochineal,* that lives on cactus out west.

Carolyn dyes only a small part of her wool. As soon as she returns with her flowers, she puts her dye material in a *bath* and simmers it in an enamel pot on a small gas burner by the driveway's edge. While the dye material (or *dyestuff*) simmers, Carolyn puts the yarn in another pot with a mixture of simmering water and alum or chrome, which are both chemicals. This process *mordants* the wool; that is, it makes it ready to accept the dye. After mordanting, the wool is immersed in the dye bath and begins to take on color.

A BLANKET FOR MAX

Summer turns to fall, and the days grow shorter. Sunlight pours through Carolyn's window, but even sunlight on shortening days cannot compete with the excitement of an idea. And so Carolyn will stay inside on this bright morning, to weave.

Last night the idea for the design of a small blanket came to her and she planned it while she was lying in bed. It would be a simple blanket using white wool from Henry, gray wool from Strawberry, and dark brown wool from Amy. The blanket would be about thirty-seven or thirty-eight inches wide and about fifty inches long. Carolyn would use a *plain-weave* pattern, also called a *basket weave,* in which the *weft* threads, the horizontal ones, are woven over-under-over-under the *warp* threads, which are the vertical threads that form the foundation for the weft's over-under path. Carolyn was so excited that she got out of bed to *dress the loom* so that she could begin weaving first thing in the morning.

Each warp thread is guided through the *heddles,* a small set of metal strips that hang in a harness across the loom, and then are fastened. When the heddles are raised by pumping the *foot treadles,* various warp threads are lifted for the weft to be woven through. The order in which the heddles are raised decides the pattern of the wool fabric. Carolyn will raise the heddles in a certain order to make the basket-weave pattern.

It takes Carolyn hours to thread the hundreds of heddles. By the time she finishes it is after midnight.

The first thing she does the next morning is to put a skein of Henry's white wool on the *swift* and wind it onto the *ski shuttle,* which will shuttle the weft thread through the warp. The swift is an instrument for winding yarn into a ball or onto a shuttle. This swift is made of wood and looks like a crown with a complicated configuration of interlocking x's, triangles, and diamonds. Carolyn drops on the swift a skein of yarn spun from Henry's wool and begins winding it off onto her ski shuttle. The swift spins round and round, making a low groan like a small animal as it turns. Soon Carolyn has enough yarn on her shuttle to begin weaving.

First Carolyn's feet touch lightly on the loom's treadles. The heddles raise and with them come waves of countless warp threads. The *shed* is open. This is a space in the warp, a tunnel through which Carolyn can slide the ski shuttle. A light push from Carolyn, and the ski slides across the warp carrying its weft. There is a sound like a wind whisper with an occasional wooden knock as the ski glides through the threads to the loom's other side.

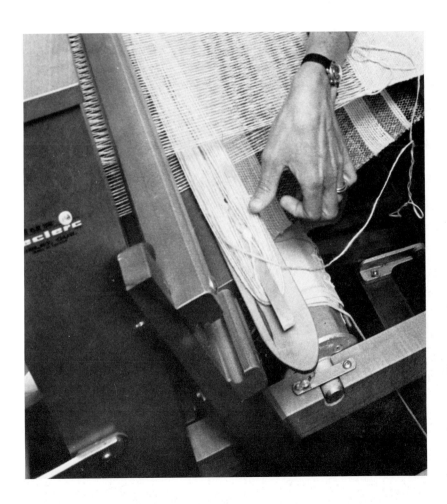

The ski is through. Carolyn reaches for the wooden *beater bar* and packs the newly woven weft thread firmly against the warp. There is a dry sandy sound as the horizontal weft threads lock into the vertical warp ones. Carolyn's feet change treadles. Different heddles are raised. A new shed is opened. The ski takes off. The beater packs.

There are at least three different kinds of wood sounds — *clicks, clacks,* and hollow *tocks* as the loom is worked. And there are soft and sandy sounds as the beater bar packs the weft. But, as Carolyn weaves on, a pattern of wool and wood sounds begins to emerge.

In ten minutes Carolyn has woven two inches. Her shoulders are beginning to ache. For days in August she has scrambled up hillsides collecting plants. She has felt the backs of her arms grow sore from the first day of carding and then grow stronger on the following days. Now a new set of muscles are hurting. Carolyn figures that by the time she is halfway through weaving the blanket, at twenty-five or thirty inches, her shoulder muscles will be accustomed to the strain.

Later, as she sits with Max, allowing him to weave a tiny bit of blanket, Carolyn suddenly realizes who the blanket would suit best. For Carolyn, this moment is as exciting as when the first lambs are born in March.

THE WEAVER'S GIFT

Carolyn has worked all day on the blanket. Just before dinner she completes the last inches and cuts the blanket from the loom. She knots the warp ends so that the blanket will not fray and twists these ends into tassels. Then she washes the blanket to make it soft and spreads it out to dry.

The first frost is still five weeks off, but the baby lamb born six long months before, on a raw March morning, now has a fleece that has thickened and makes his body look chubby and round and ready for the coldest Vermont winter. Carolyn calls Max's mother on the phone and tells her she has a winter gift for her son.

Next morning Max and his mother arrive. The bold stripes of the blanket catch Max's eyes. Carolyn barely has time to say "For you, Max!" before the little boy has picked it up. His tiny hands move lightly over the woven blanket, which still has a slight feel of oil. Then he presses his face against it. The more he touches the blanket, the more excited he becomes. He throws it in the air and catches it and then rubs his cheek against it once more. He burrows under it like an animal making a nest. He plays peek-a-boo and ghost and Indian. Max has never felt anything like this blanket. It feels springy, thrilling, and almost alive. But, most of all, it feels special—more than just wool has been woven into this blanket. It is the weaver's gift.

CAROLYN and MILTON FRYE live on a small farm in Norwich, Vermont. Milton is the principal of the Norwich elementary school and Carolyn, a former nursery school teacher, is now devoting her time to weaving.

KATHRYN LASKY and CHRISTOPHER G. KNIGHT live in Cambridge, Massachusetts, with their young son, Max (who appears in *The Weaver's Gift*). They also have a house in Vershire, Vermont.

Ms. Lasky is the author of several children's books, including *My Island Grandma*, published by Warne in 1979. She and her husband, a former photographer for *National Geographic*, have collaborated on three previously published books for young readers: *I Have Four Names for my Grandfather, Tugboats Never Sleep,* and *Tall Ships.*

The Knights have twice sailed their own small boat across the Atlantic Ocean.